Man Overbored

Cliff Hardy was bored. Here he was, sitting in his sailboat in the Caribbean on a full moon romantic night, alone.

He sighed, and read the titles of the books on the little shelf. All about voodoo and zombies and that kind of stuff.

Well, he was near enough to Jamaica and Haiti, where that stuff was practiced.

He was bored. He was there. What if...?

Contents

About the author

CD Moulton has traveled extensively over much of the world both in the music business, where he was a rock guitarist, songwriter and arranger and in an import/export business. He has been everything from a bar owner to auto salvage (junkyard) manager, longshoreman to high steel worker, orchid grower to landscaper, tropical fish farmer to commercial fisherman. He started writing books in 1983 and has published more than 350 books as of January 1, 2023. His most popular books to date are about research with orchids, though much of his science fiction and fantasy work has proven popular. He wrote the CD Grimes, PI series, and the Det. Nick Storie series, Clint Faraday series, and many other works.

He now resides in Gualaca, Chiriqui, Panamá, where he writes books, plays music with friends, does research with orchids and medicinal plants. He has lately become involved in fighting for the rights of the indigenous people, who are among his closest friends, and in fighting the extreme corruption in the courts and police in Panamá.

He offers the free e-book, *Fading Paradise*, that explains what he has been through because of the corruption.

CD is the discoverer of the Chadam Protocol for curing cancer.

Facebook page Ambrosia peruviana for cancer.

Man Overbored

Romantic Nights – Yeah! Right!

Cliff Hardy looked up at the huge bright perfect romantic full golden moon over the Caribbean and sighed.

Romantic moon. Yeah, right! His romantic life was non-existent! Here he was, the perfect place, at the perfect time, with the perfect conditions. It was a dream time that lacked only one small barely significant thing: the female.

He sighed again, grimaced, and threw the three-quarters of a bottle of Corona overboard. He usually relaxed with a Corona every night at this time, but nothing appealed to him. Nothing.

What a lousy damned mood!

Well, read something. He did have that way to pass the time. The only thing wrong with that was he'd read everything except the few books about Caribbean witchcraft and gory paranormal events that were supposed to be real. That crap had never much appealed to him. He was spending a lot of time down here in the places it was practiced. Jamaica, Haiti, Dominica. He'd met two authors who did "research" on those subjects who were totally convinced it was real. He'd met papalois, voodoo priests, who could do things he couldn't explain, but a lot of it was theater.

If there was only something that could bring a few minutes of excitement into his life, now was the time.

He looked over the little shelf with the witchcraft references, and sighed again. He grabbed one at random and thumbed through to the index. He was in this near area, so looked at the chapter on voodoo as practiced in Haita.

He read for about an hour. He sort of got into it in places, because he knew the incident. This was one of the authors he'd met, and the one case was something he knew about. "D. F. G. Hunter" wasn't his real name, of course. Cliff knew him as Gordon. He said the nom de plume initials stood for Damned Fucking Ghost.

Gordy had believed in what was happening, then. Two years ago. He sent this book just half a year ago, because Cliff was in it. Cliff thought it was all theater and prestidigitation. Regardless, it was weird.

Gordy was living on a little out-island. He could drop by and maybe find some new thing going on that would interest him. Gordy had a hot girlfriend who could hook him up to ... damn it, no more whores! That's what his life was about for the past four years, and he was sick of it! He wanted a woman he could talk to, and maybe even care about. The last six or eight airheads had been no better than masturbation! It reminded him of a line in a book he'd read. The guy found himself laying all alone in the bed with a woman. That's what it was like with them. All alone in bed with them.

It was only about eighty two nautical miles to where Gordy was staying now. He was wandering, so it didn't matter where he went.

He thought the worst thing that had happened in his life was when he inherited four million dollars. He'd always dreamed of owning a sleek sailboat and spending his time in exotic ports with exotic women. He did that, and found it was truly great, if you took almost any one night out, but adding them in chronological order was B-O-O-R-R-I-I-N-N-G-G!

He finished the chapter, and sat back to think. He remembered the bodies that had washed up on the beach, without a mark on them. Emile said they were zombies that had wandered into the salt water. Salt kills zombies.

Sure! Four zombies wearing life vests wandered into the ocean!

Cliff suspected they were political rivals of some slimewad, which there were a lot of in politics in that part of the Caribbean, even more, if you could accept it, than in regular politics.

Well, maybe he could find some excitement here. He had a small glimmer of an idea.

Whatever, it could wait until morning. He sacked out.

<u>*Smooth Sailing*</u>

The wind was moderate to light enough for Cliff to make steady if slow progress toward Isla Lunatica. He spent a lot of time putting things together and in order. He would stop on the way, in Port Au Prince, for supplies and whatever took his fancy. He liked to have fifty percent more food and water aboard than he was likely to use. He bought a lot of new clothes, but of the type he wore. No more suits or fancy shoes. Tee shirts and shorts and jeans and tank tops with flip flops or Crocks. Bathing suits. He was well enough built and in good enough condition that he could wear the Bikini types, though he thought thongs were just plain vulgar. Most men nowadays were fat and out of shape, and looked purely disgusting in Bikinis, or even boxer types. A big floppy gut hanging over – you wanted to puke!

The women were as bad, a lot of the ones from the states or Canada or much of Europe. Fifty pounds overweight, and wearing a string Bikini. It was enough to make you swear lifetime celibacy! He remembered that nude beach in

Mexico. You thought you were on the set of "My Horrible Sexual Nightmare!" or something.

Well, he wasn't interested to the extent he'd even consider half that extreme, right now. He had regular periods of excess horniness, and other periods of not much caring. That nude beach had started in his high horniness stage and had gone to no interest whatever in an hour.

He ran into a group of Rastas, and chatted for a minute. One was a white with the dredlocks and all. He looked ridiculous. He tried to talk the Wadi-Wadi and Patois, but didn't pull it off. Cliff caught a smirk on one of the Rasta's faces, and grinned. He got the rubbing fingers that told him the jerk was tolerated because he was paying the bills. He turned back toward him, and caught him staring at his crotch. He raised an eyebrow at the Rasta, and got a small nod. He was introduced to Billy. Billy seemed to be a nice enough guy, in a lot of ways.

It wasn't anything to him. He got into a sort of "What if?" thought pattern as he walked toward the dock and his boat. That guy would probably end up washing ashore somewhere, without a mark on him, if he ran out of money around the voodoo types.

He was probably actually a nice enough guy. Gordy felt he was. He just tried too hard. He was the type people would like if he'd drop the act and phony front. The gay part was a non-issue, in most of these parts.

There were half a dozen kids on the dock by his boat, but none had gone aboard. He had a fancy voodoo figure hanging over the gangplank. He put a bit of sugar on his finger as he went aboard, and touched the finger to the mouth of the figure, and said, "Merci mon ami."

"Where'd you get the juju, mon?" a kid asked.

"Mama Bernadine. Kingston."

"Downharbor?"

"Downharbor in."

The kid nodded. "Very scary. She be powerful! We goes aboard 'n we don't never come back off in our real minds!"

"Not that bad, but something like that. You spend seven years, seven months, seven days, seven hours, and seven minutes scared of your own shadow, and with plenty good reason! Your shadow trips you and strangles you all the time. Got to be where you don't got no shadow."

"Not easy, mon. Not easy."

Cliff gave them all candy and a nickel apiece. When he came back they would watch his boat for him. Nothing would be stolen.

Voodoo was a powerful force, here, real or not! Use it, but with the greatest care.

He chatted with the kids a bit, then went aboard as they went happily off the dock to spend their nickels. He grinned to himself, and went inside. He puttered around a bit, then dozed for awhile. He had those little spotty dreams you can't quite remember. That Billy character was in them, some of the time. Something ... the gay bit? Cliff never cared for that, but ... it was lost. Why would he dream of that? He'd never been fucked, but it was in the dream. Billy was in his bed ... it was gone.

He thought about the strange ways that your subconscious could be trying to tell you something. Maybe he was attracted to Billy, on some level he wasn't aware of.

He moved away from the dock and set his sails. He would go slow, and would read a lot more of the occult things. He couldn't believe he became so interested in it, but there was a lot of information that fit a lot of situations that had nothing to do with voodoo. It was basically a philosophy, not a true religion. The religion was added because some sordid people thought it was a good way to hold personal power, or to get a few dishonest dollars. Religion, as usual, was what brought in the theatrics.

Religion and politics. Two things that divided people and set them against each other. Most things brought people together.

Cliff moved out into the open Caribbean and dropped a drift anchor. He would spend time reading those occult books. Maybe he would crank up his computer, which he seldom did, anymore, and do a little research. He could go to Gordy's with some knowledge. Maybe there would be something weird he could study with Gordy. Anything that would break up the total boredom with a too-perfect life was a positive.

He studied about making various jujus, such as the one that Mama Bernadine had made for him. He'd gotten along very well with the big happy pudgy woman who dressed in unbelievably bright colors and wore big mirrored sunglasses – and liked her rum.

She had made the figure out of straw and fibers and a lot of really disgusting things. He had said it was a doll. It couldn't do anything!

"It don't matter none wot it do. It matter plenty wot people *think* it do!"

That's why they got along. Not a big bullshit line. Just the basic fact: it's about suggestion.

They'd gotten pretty drunk together, and he'd asked her how she got started in the voodoo bit. She said she was a little girl, and her mama knew a little voodoo medicine. People said she had the evil eye, because she had been mad at another little girl a year older than her, and a lot bigger. The girl had called her ugly, and had slapped her when she said the girl didn't know what ugly was. When she was a year older, she would know.

"I did some silly signs with the fingers, mon. It was only a child being mean to another child. Wot happen, there is this fire, and she done got her face burned one side that was all scars thenafter, mon. In three months, me supposed curse come true. I done played it for wot 'twas worth. I'd claim I could put a curse on anybody wot said anything mean about me, mon.

"Two years later, a man who called me a little whore, I was six years old! He done got a stingray stab in his foot 'n it got infected 'n he done died horrible. Everbody was scairt to death of me! It were a powerful feelin, mon! Never had to do nought since. Here, I'm thirty four, and ain't never had to do nothin' but say don't fuck with me, mon, you die horrible!

"'Course, it done got a down side, mon. Ain't nobody gonna love Mama Bernadine! That stuff always sooner or later done got over, then wot? I gonna put a horror death spell on you?

"Mama Bernadine done found her glass empty, mon!"

Cliff liked these simple people. He saw from

his reading that it really was suggestion, to a great degree. Suggestion could be a powerful thing. It even worked on people who didn't know they believed in whatever spell was supposed to be working on them. There were a lot of cases where that was shown.

Four days. He had made jujus out of seaweed and big fish scales and sharks teeth and such. He could use his old clothes to make things that were more like good luck charms.

He studied poisons, but there wasn't much on how to produce the really scary things. Cyanide and such, he already knew quite a lot about. Belladona, *Amanita muscaria,* casaba, puffer fish toxin, sea urchins. A lot of things you had to know about if you lived on the sea.

He was going to lose interest now. He'd studied it all, and going over and over a thing was back to boredom.

He set sail for Isla Lunatica.

Cliff noted the people standing around near the dock at Gordy's place as he came into the island. They seemed excited and jumpy. He asked Gordy what was going on when he came to greet him.

"Oh, some kind of voodoo curse or something, right here. They think it's against me, because I delve into their superstitions."

"What the hell does that mean? What happened to get them like this?"

"A body on the beach, right where my stream runs into the ocean."

"A body? So? Is it a voodoo thing that you study, so they hooked it to you?"

"Not until it disappeared."

"It ... disappeared? What?"

"Some of the kids saw it caught on a limb, or something. They wouldn't go near. They came to tell their parents and me about it. When we went back, it was gone. They think it was a sea zombie that came to warn me about something."

"You didn't see it, yet it was to warn you? Maybe the kids made it up."

"I was about to say that, but every damned one of them have a Blackberry, it seems. They don't know where their next meal will come from, but they have a damned hundred fifty dollar cell phone, for Christ's sake! They have pictures. It was definitely there an hour and a half ago. It was as definitely gone half an hour ago."

"One of the island blacks who got drunk and fell, right then, the kids ran to tell you, he got up and went on."

"No footprints. It wasn't a black. It was some guy with a long Rasta hair braid. Blond. Wearing a life vest and khaki pants.

"Jorge! Ven aca!"

A kid, about twelve years old, came over. Gordy said to show Cliff the pictures of the body. He explained that Jorge had the sense to use the zoom, and had some fairly clear pictures.

Cliff studied the body, what he could see. It was caught on some kind of small driftwood branch that Gordy said was still there. Its back was toward the camera, There were long blond Rasta braids, probably down to the lower shoulder blades. It seemed to be a man of about "normal" size, wearing an orange life vest. There seemed to be some red on the right shoulder, which was up. Cliff asked about it.

"I think it was just a red bandana. You can zoom it a little before it pixelates, and it has sharp edges. It's not blood.

There were no footprints found close. He came from the water, and returned to the water. It ... what's that.... There was something on the end of the limb?"

"Here." Gordy took a seaweed figure from the shelf on the fish cleaning sink.

"It's a juju? That's what makes them think it's a voodoo curse against you?"

"I have to study the juju. How it was made will tell me what it was supposed to accomplish."

Gordy introduced Cliff to several of the people, then they drifted off to go back to work, or whatever. They would have something to talk about today, at least.

"Come on up to the house. I want to check out some references on this thing. I can't think of why anyone would want to curse me, but you never know.

"Henrietta! Company! We could use some hot strong coffee!"

The attractive young girl who was Gordy's present live-in waved, and went inside. Gordy brought the juju to the door, and she said he was not going to cross the threshold with that thing! He grinned, and sat it in the rocking chair, then they went inside for strong coffee and fishcakes. Gordy took his laptop onto the porch and brought up some files on jujus. He studied them for awhile, and shook his head.

"What?"

"It's a thing that says I am not to do something or other in the sea. It seems the body was only a projection of the juju, and that it has returned to the juju, meaning it's right here!

"I don't get it! It was there with this hanging on the driftwood right over it! It shouldn't have been there when the body was there. It *was* the body!"

"I don't get it, either. This doesn't look much like that body in the picture."

"That's what puzzles me. It does. It's damned good.

"A projection ... here. See this strand of blond hair woven into the head? It's projected as a full head of hair, like the one it was taken from. This tiny patch of orange? It's from a life vest the maker of the juju had worn. The same is true for the khaki pants. It's pretty exact. If we could see the face of the body, it would be the face of the one who made the juju. He used his own things. Hair, clothes.

"See this little phallus woven into the head? The maker is gay. It's a black phallus, so he likes black men. Maybe that's why the blond Rasta hair. He would hang out with the Rastas."

"Jesus! Billy!"

"Jesus Billy?"

"I met a guy in Haiti who had blond dredlocks, and was gay. He was hanging out with the Rastas. He seemed a nice enough person, but not very smart to be pulling that act. I figured he wanted to be accepted, and was buying friends."

"But ... why would ... voodoo? It ... I never met anyone like that! Why would he put a curse on me?"

"So the juju is a curse? Definitely?"

"Well, it could just be a warning. Actually, it could be a friendly warning, of some sort, but why would a perfect stranger be warning me about ... what?"

"It looks like you really have a puzzle with this one! It's sort of scary, in another way. I met the guy, once, on the dock in Haiti. Why would this thing come here when I was coming here? I didn't even mention you."

"There are reasons. We have to find what they are."

"We?"

"It would seem to me that you're a definite connection. Too much coincidence for you not to be."

"Yeah. I meet this turkey, then come here, three or four days later, there's this juju, I'm the only one who could tell you where it came from ... I think it may be a warning ... but about the sea?

"Okay. It's got my attention! I was looking for something to break up the boredom. Maybe this can do that!"

They checked a lot more, then Gordy got some books, and even communicated with a professor at a college he was working with. The only thing added was that it was a friendly warning. The juju had a small smile for a mouth.

They went down to Cliff's boat. He had left the figure hanging over the gangplank. Gordy said that thing gave him the creeps.

"It damned well works! I've never had a thing stolen from this boat!"

"It doesn't have any power of its own. I could feel it."

"Its power is the power that people think it has. Bernadine said that."

"She's a crafty one! She has half the people in Haiti and Jamaica – even Dominica – scared purely shitless of her. She's actually a rather nice person."

"She has a great sense of humor, even about herself. I like her."

"I do too. I wonder if she could tell me what this is about."

"She doesn't have any actual power. She just plays to the gallery. They all *think* she does."

"She has a psy power, I believe. I feel it. She isn't aware of it. If she'd actually studied voodoo, she would have found it. I sometimes wonder what she would be like if she knew it."

"I doubt she'd be much different. Maybe she'd have a boyfriend, now and then. They're afraid of her, now. She says that's the downside of what people think. If a guy gets interested and they have a fling, then she decides she doesn't like him anymore, will he die a horrible death?"

They chatted. Gordy said he had to wait to be able to contact certain people who were more expert about local voodoo practices. This was possibly from an earlier time when there were certain rituals that were a lot different than now. Cliff had to agree. The oldest of his books were from the late forties, and there were a number of things that had changed, drastically.

"I heard that there's some kind of deal with those Blackberries that's causing some kind of stink with Legbaon," Cliff said.

"It's inevitable. Those cults will grab at anything to have a little more power. They can use the faster communication innovations to seem to know things before anyone else. They can see a developing trend, and can predict it. Wow! How did he *know* that? Guess fifty times wrong, and once right, and they remember the one time. It's always been that way. It's what keeps psychics in business."

There wasn't any argument about that!

Cliff changed the subject. "This is a beautiful island."

Cliff stayed aboard for the night, and went to the house for breakfast. He saw the juju was inside, and asked Henrietta why.

"It be good juju."

"Gordy thinks it's a warning to help him."

"Yes. It make him safer. It warn if danger close. Liam Fontaine come today to read and see."

"Liam Fontaine? Didn't he write a book about African influence on religion here?"

"Maybe. Gordy know a lot of people who write books. He be here soon."

Gordy came out, and they chatted. Fontaine was in the area, and he contacted him. He would be there in an hour or so.

They walked around the property until the boat came to the dock. A man who looked to Cliff like a college professor came up to hail Gordy. Cliff was introduced to Dr. Fontaine, better known as Liam. Gordy and Cliff explained what they knew about the juju. Gordy said he was puzzled about several things, but it had worked.

They went to closely inspect the strange figure.

Liam used an old-fashioned magnifying glass that made Cliff think of Sherlock Holmes.

"It has no power!" Liam exclaimed, when he first touched it. "I can't believe it ever projected anything. Are you sure, or was it just what people said?"

"They took pictures with their Blackberries. It was there. There were no footprints. It was gone, and this was on the branch when I got there. I downloaded Jorge's onto the computer.

"I have but one serious question with this, as I understand this kind of juju. Why was it hanging there on that branch while the body was being projected?"

"Oh, that can happen. I've heard that Doctor Viktor can make them that do that. It means they have two purposes.

"Gordon, this may be the first time a projection was photographed! You realize that?"

"It crossed my mind."

"Why is there no power in it, now? I'm sensitive, and it doesn't seem to have anything at all.

"I see the blond hair. There is a bit of orange canvas, here, and some khaki. I know how it was made, but I don't have the ability to make it act. There have been only a few who had the ability. All of them I know about are blacks.

"I was reading a little last night about these things," Cliff said. "I think that Murdock person said they can be made in a way that the demon can go when the purpose was over, or something. Maybe it served its purpose, and left."

"Murdock? He was one of those in the fifties, wasn't he? Wrote about possessions and that kind of thing. Everything was a demon or angel. My studies haven't found either. It's a power some people have," Liam argued.

"That's not to say a person using the power can't produce that kind of thing," Gordy replied. "I find it most intriguing, but not because of that!"

"Yes. What was the possible purpose? If it was to warn you about a future event, it hasn't been accomplished until the event is past!"

"So what was changed because of this juju between when it was first seen until ten minutes ago?" Gordy asked.

They looked at each other, and they all shrugged.

"Well ... I know of one thing," Cliff said. "I was planning to get Gordy to go to Pearl Island this morning. We didn't go? It's in the sea, so would fit, I guess."

"We must see what has happened between here

and there!" Gordy cried. He took out his satellite cell phone and punched a speed-dial number. They waited for half a minute, then Gordy said, "Henri? Gordon here. What happened out there last night?"

It was on speaker. "I'll never know how you voodoo people know about these things! I'll never know!

"Other than that a drug boat was run down in the bay by the US Coast Guard, and four people were shot, nothing. Two boats were shot up a bit, because the runner tried to keep them between, but they weren't damaged, much. No one was on deck, or there might have been casualties."

"Thanks, Henri. Tell Amanda I said hello." He rang off.

"Well! If you had been there, and on the deck of the boat, you might well have been shot. The juju made you not go. Its purpose was served. The power left the juju then, because it was no longer required," Liam said. "I might actually study about the demons I don't believe in!"

They laughed and joked awhile about demons and angels, and what Liam called residual power eddies.

"Well! Mystery solved!" Liam declared.

"No. It is just begun," Gordy replied. "Who is

this Billy, and how did he know, where did he get the power, why would he want to protect someone he never met?

"I think perhaps we should go to Haiti and ask him, don't you?"

"Maybe he has a psychic power, and doesn't have any idea how he knew, or why he did it," Cliff suggested. "I was there, and there was some kind of psychic ... Gordy, how did he get that juju *here*? There are a lot of questions I don't think I want answers to! This is downright weird!"

"It is intriguing. I think there isn't any danger," Liam replied. "He sent a protection. That doesn't seem so sinister as many of these things are. The question I have is what the connection is.

"Gordon, have you ever done a favor of any magnitude for any truly powerful practitioner of these arts?"

"I suppose I have, but nothing distinct comes to mind. Why?"

"Displacement. What happens when you go to Haiti and this Billy person has no memory of any part of it?"

"Displacement?" Cliff asked. That wasn't in any of the books he read. Too many things he'd never considered were showing up. Too many coincidences that couldn't be coincidences.

"It's mostly hypnotism. Whenever a powerful priest wants to do something where it is important no one knows he did whatever, he can find a subject, hypnotize him, and have him make the juju or whatever. He puts the power into it and delivers it, no one knows he sent it.

"What this entails, then, is that the priest was involved in the drug shipment and his power told him you were going to be in deadly danger. He prevented that happening. He wouldn't want it traced to him, because he is involved with drugs. You see?"

"Or maybe he caused the interception of the drugs. Same applies. He wouldn't want it to be known he was involved," Gordy said.

They discussed a lot of possible scenarios. Cliff thought they got a little too far out with some of them. There was a lot here that had him confused. He wasn't sure he wanted answers to a large part of it. It didn't seem too possible. How had he gotten involved with this voodoo stuff? How much power did people actually have? Was this Liam Fontaine character, who had two Phd's, really sensitive to some kind of psychic power?

He actually had been planning on going to Pearl Island. How much power did he have that he didn't even suspect – before?

It was bullshit! Mama Bernadine had put it right there on the line! It wasn't what power any of these things had, it was what power people *thought* they had that worked! Suggestion, pure and simple!

But...?

Fontaine was going back to a little island, not far away, where he was studying a girl who had the power to affect his computer screen. He was fascinated, because she was learning how to do more than cause static patterns and lines and streaks.

Gordy wanted to go to Haiti. If Cliff didn't want to go, he would take his own boat. He wanted to meet this Billy character to see if he really did or didn't know he had made a juju that worked. If he didn't, he was determined to find out who caused him to make it. Liam had suggested, it was probably someone directly involved in a drug deal, one side or the other, and someone couldn't have it known he was in any way involved in that. Considering what Gordy said about Mama Bernadine having a lot of the power – but not knowing it – was scary. Considering what had happened, he wondered if he had some power he wasn't aware of.

He hoped not. He could live without being

some kind of stupid psychic medium. They were a bunch of creeps, the ones he'd met. Misfits who had a racket going.

A few of them were okay. Those were mostly the ones like Mama Bernadine. They had a good sense of humor about themselves. They weren't always trying to scare everyone around them into anything.

Well, he hadn't been in Haiti long, and several days had gone by. Probably Billy wasn't even there, anymore. If he was, Liam had given him a reason not to know anything, but it still involved someone pretty powerful to have caused what had happened. It was all confusing and scary. Cliff didn't want to be involved with those powers anymore. He was flippant and worse about them, a day ago. Now he was getting worried about them. It seemed you didn't know what angle they were coming from.

He said he was ready to go to Haiti. They could use the time en route to study this whole mess, and try to figure out what was going on. That something was didn't seem to be questionable.

Gordy went to the house to get some things together while Cliff rigged the boat for the open water. There was a little cloud bank between there and Haiti, but it didn't seem the kind of thing that would cause any real problems. Radar didn't show anything too extreme.

They set off. They would arrive in Port Au Prince tomorrow, about noon, if the wind held well. It was good leisurely sailing weather. No one would win a race with the conditions, but it made for a pleasant trip.

Just before dark, the cloud bank was close. It didn't look bad, but Cliff got on the weather channel again to see it was a narrow band, moving slowly westward. There weren't any bad spots on the radar or satellite pictures.

They watched the light rain falling soon after dark. The winds were moderate, and only as they passed into the band. It looked like pretty smooth sailing until just before dawn, when they would pass out of the band. Gordy would take first watch, and he would take second. He was used to sleeping early and waking up in time to watch the sunrise. He would just be getting up three hours before normal.

It was just fifteen minutes after he took over the watch that the violent little storm cell hit them. He yelled to Gordy, and they had to fight the sails down. Cliff dropped the drag anchor to keep them headed into the storm, and fought the side gusts for more than an hour. He was exhausted when they were finally past the cell.

He went in to the radar and checked.

Strange! There was no cell detected.

He ran the data-form back to the point they entered the violent cell. It didn't show on the radar. He did a fast forward until the moment. Radar had never picked up the cell.

Gordy came in from getting the sails ready to hoist, and saw the screen. Cliff told him that cell was never on radar. They had been in it for more than an hour. It had to be three miles across, but never showed.

Gordy ran the radar info through like Cliff had. There was never a cell shown.

"It gets weirder and weirder," Cliff said. "It's past, so I'm going to sack out for about an hour. I'm dead exhausted. We can ride the anchor and hoist when I'm able to move again!"

Gordy agreed. He'd be in the second bunk.

They went into the bunkroom. Cliff squealed, and pointed to the bed. Mama Bernadine's juju was there, on his pillow.

"Oh, yeah. I found it blown up against the cabin entrance and put it there."

"Ghee! Don't you ever do anything like that to me again!" Cliff demanded, then got the giggles. Gordy also started giggling. They laughed until their lungs ached. Cliff finally sobbed that he needed a little sleep one hell of a lot more than he even guessed.

They sacked out. It was more like four hours before they woke up and hoisted the sails.

At least, the boredom was down on the scale for awhile!

They came into port at just before four in the afternoon. As they tied to the dock, the kids from before came running to greet them. Cliff had the juju hanging over the gangplank again. He did the routine with the sugar on his finger as he and Gordy went ashore. He gave the kids nickels, and they would watch the boat, but said it was too easy a job. The juju was watching. One of the kids asked what the juju's name was, and he said, "Azterifat," off the top of his head. The kid looked serious, and said they liked that kind of name.

As they walked along the dock, Cliff said, "I think I'm getting superstitious."

"What do you mean?"

"Azterifat. I think that name'll stick. I just added two and two and got twenty two, where the juju's concerned."

"I don't get it, at all. Mama Bernadine has some power, but she doesn't know it. She couldn't give any to the juju."

"I sometimes use the sugar ritual – when those kids are around or someone else is who might believe in that stuff. I just noticed something.

"I used it the last few times I left a port, or got to a port. It was always smooth sailing. I forgot it twice, and had problems, both times. First one was a month or so ago. I ran into a little sandbar that wasn't supposed to be in that area. It was deep water. This time, I didn't do it when we left your dock, and we run into a storm that wasn't there. I don't think I'll want to take any chances by not doing it anytime I leave or arrive anywhere.

"When I left here, before, I did it. The weather was perfect! I anchored out for a few days, then went to your place. I was hoisting the sails for your place, and passed under Azterifat, and sort of automatically put the sugar on my finger for him. It was perfect until I left your dock."

Gordy laughed, and said he'd seen some very scary things, so he wasn't about to argue. What harm would it do to do the sugar routine when he left or arrived at a port?

"Better safe than sorry, trite as it is."

"There's another thing. When that kid asked its name, that came to me. Azterifat. I knew, right then, its name was Azterifat. It's as positive as I know your name's Gordon."

"If you're trying to scare me, I think it's starting to work."

They joked a bit, then went into town. The Rastas from before were at a little cantina. He asked about Billy.

"That dude? He were gone day after you was here. Sort'a sorry. He still had plenty money, mon!

"He were weird, but he were alright good, in his way. Good fuck, 'n most gays aren't, you know?"

"He liked the stick?" Gordy asked.

"He more'n liked it! He were good."

They laughed, and went on. Cliff asked about other people who had been there he'd met. A Frenchman from "PairEE, eh mon ami?" who was still around. He was sitting on the porch of a pension with three rather obvious pros. All he could talk about was partying with them all night and most of the day.

"A sex god, in his own mind," Gordy said, as they went on. "I'll bet he's never had a piece in his life he didn't pay for."

They went more into the section Gordy was interested in. There were two witch women there he'd spent time studying. He said Lizette had some power, but Gina didn't.

They went to Mama Lizette's place, and in, passing through three sets of hanging draperies into a dark room with a lot of big red candles supplying what light there was. Mama Lizette was a thin, craggy older woman. She could be forty or she could be eighty. The place smelled of incense and marijuana.

Lizette took one look at Cliff, and said, "Why you bring that one here? Why he hide the power? He think Mama Lizette not see he got power? What he want here?"

"He's a friend. I don't think he has any power. I've never felt it," Gordy replied.

She stared at him, closed her eyes, and did a little spin, made some signs, and jumped, slightly.

"It ain't his none of his power. Power about him from someone. It not agin me. It not ... agin nobody. It got ... a protection in with it."

She spun and started making odd noises. She twisted, and came to within inches of his face.

"Mon, go from here!" she cried. "It a power ... it not good, but it not bad! It a wild power, but it not you! Go! Go!"

Gordy grabbed his arm, and led him out.

"Gordy!" she screamed. He stopped. "Yes?"

"No cemetery! No go near cemetery! You never leave! What you got on you what got the curse? What somebody give you what got a curse?"

She came out, and passed her hand around

him. She stopped by his left front pocket. "It there. It a call. I take away it power. Give me it."

He shrugged, and emptied his pocket. There was a little amethyst bead. He said he didn't have a clue as to how it got there. She took it, put it on the little table, made a couple of passes with her hands over it, and snapped her fingers.

"It done dead. No more call." She handed it to Gordy. It was a little grey rock.

Cliff grinned at her. She said, "I done told you to go from here! Go!"

They went out. Gordy said that was a weird experience. It wasn't the first he'd had with her.

"She's a fake. I saw her drop the rock in your pocket, and I watched her palm the pink one and hand you that rock. She's good, but I studied about how it was done. The gobbledegook was to distract you."

"Oh, that. I know. I saw it the first time I came here. I mean about the power someone put in you to protect me.

"Cliff, I'm putting this thing together. I have to find the clues, because it's like Liam said. You were used, somehow, and don't know it. It has to be tied in with that projection at my place. This Billy character is a lot more important than we can guess, but how?

"Cliff, I need to know everything you know about him. He's the key. Describe him, as close as you can."

"Well, he was about eighteen or nineteen, pretty good build, slender, but powerful. Like he lifted weights. Maybe five ten or eleven, and one sixty. Yellow/blond hair that was braided Rasta and hung just below his shoulder blades. Very good teeth. I noticed – why did I think of that? – that he had your nose and eyes.

"I didn't even notice his eyes! What's going on?"

"I see. Did he speak with an accent?"

Cliff thought about it. He was getting really scared, now. "Yes, a sort of Southern accent, with a tiny bit of ... Jamaica?"

"Cajun?"

"Well, I don't remember ever hearing Cajun. It could be. Why? Was ... oh! New Orleans, and the voodoo there?"

"Cliff, I think you met my son. I think he's trying to protect me. I think I even know who his mother is. She was the most powerful person I had ever met, at the time. I cared for her, and I think she cared for me, but she made me go, after about three weeks.

"Now I have more incentive than ever to meet Billy. I also need to know how he was able to transplace power to you. That usually means entering your body. He never was in a position to do that, I don't think?"

Cliff remembered the dream. With all this, it was no dream.

"Gordy, I think he fucked me. Would that do it?"

"You think? He fucked you?"

"I thought it was a dream. He came onto the boat, here, just before I left. I was dozing ... I ... he came aboard. I remember ... and he said some kind of ... he talked to Azterifat! I remember, he came on board, and that Azterifat was there ... something. He just came toward me, and I don't remember anything much, except I thought I was dreaming. He did some things, and ... he said this wouldn't hurt, that it would be pleasant, then he fucked me. It *was* pleasant! It felt like we were one body, somehow. He said ... that Mama loved her man for life, and that she would keep him from harm and evil.

"Gordy, I don't know what's happening! I'm scared!

"I made the so-called projection out of old clothes, and some old curtains the color of his hair. I put a ... Gordy, I never thought about it! I thought I was making a sort of joke thing, where you would have to investigate, and the boredom would end, for a little while!

"I had a little of his hair to put on the figure! I never asked myself where I got it!"

"You didn't ask yourself how you got the figure to that branch on the beach without leaving footprints?"

"That was easy. That blue tarp, folded six layers thick, roll it onto the sand, walk on it, take it up when you get back aboard the boat. Wait until somebody finds it and leaves, then take it away the same way.

"I didn't think there would be pictures. It was just luck they weren't clear enough to show it was old clothes stuffed with more old clothes."

"You were used. You became the force in the juju, and you still have some of that inside. I hope we can use it to call my son. I want to meet him. I want to know about his mother.

"Cliff, she was the reason I decided to get my second Phd. I decided to study the paranormal sciences from a scientific base. My first was about halfway done, and this was added. I attended two universities for two years. It was two at Loyola, then two at both, then two at Smithfield.

"Maribel. She was beautiful. I fell in love with her overnight, then was ... she made me go. I knew she loved me like I loved her. This proves it. I think I never stopped loving her. Ever.

"I have to meet our son, Cliff. I have to!"

"I'm willing to try anything, at this point. I do know I've found a sure way to fight boredom, at worst!"

Cliff went back to the boat. Gordy would come later. He thought he could find where Billy had gone. He knew people who would know.

He went through the boat, where he found some things he couldn't explain. He went out on deck and talked to Azterifat.

"Azterifat, thank you for all you've done to help me and Gordy. I think you also know what's happening with Billy, and I think you know it's not bad. I think he told you he was going to fuck me, didn't he?"

He expected no response, and got none. "I'm nuts! I'm talking to a doll!

"Azterifat, I think I believe in you. I think you really do protect me. I think running onto that non-existent sandbar stopped something else from happening. I think that non-existent storm was another thing that stopped something bad from happening.

"Did Billy actually transfer a power into me when he fucked me?"

It had to be a small gust of wind, or something. Azterifat seemed to nod!

"Azterifat, will it bother Gordy much that his son is gay?"

No response.

"I know that a lot of the magic stuff has to do with sex. Is he just using sex to accomplish a goal? If so, why were those Rastas fucking him?

"I'm confused about a lot of it. I think that I remember that it felt good to be fucked, but was that because it was Billy?

"This is a mess!"

He went into the cabin. He had left a book on the counter. He was going to return it to the shelf when he noted a page was dog-eared. He didn't do that. Ever.

He opened the book to the marked page. There didn't seem to be anything there, so he went to the next page. It started a chapter: *The Role of Sex in Magic Rites*. That might tell ... how had Azterifat moved that book there, and how did Azterifat dog-ear a page?

He wasn't going to question a lot of things he always had. Not anymore!

The chapter was informative.

The researcher will come upon what seems to be an overstressed sexual part of many rites. At times, it seems that all the magic is an excuse to perform sexual acts, many of a perverted nature.

I have found that the sexual part is very much

critical to various things. The practitioner can derive much energy from those acts. He can take energy when he is on the receiving end, and can store that energy. somehow. The mechanism isn't clear to me. He passes energy when he is on the sending end, so to speak. It is a rather complex question. I have found the sexual acts are quite often definitely and unquestionably critical to certain rites, particularly the sending parts. Energy is emplaced by those acts. That energy remains under the direction of the sender.

According to the study (vol. #7, pg. 132) by Carstairs and Evans, the sender will most generally place himself on the receiving end of the energy transfer. He will join into the acts with several for the undirected input of energy to be used for one implantation of directed energy on his next sending. He will generally select very strong and positive people from whom to receive ...

That explained a lot about Billy. Perhaps Gordy knew about that, and it wouldn't bother him.

Cliff put the book on the shelf, and went to the door to say, "Thanks!" to Azterifat. He went out, and did the sugar ritual.

Gordy came aboard, about half an hour later,

and simply said, "Jamaica. Kingston." Cliff asked, "Mama Bernadine?"

"Yes."

They quickly rigged and moved away from the dock to set sail. Gordy discussed several things. Cliff asked about the homosexual parts with Billy. Gordy said he'd seen several studies that seemed to show such things did actually impart a strong psychic energy. He read the part Cliff had just read, and asked what made him look that up. Was it the fact he had been on the receiving end of such acts?

"I think Azterifat found it and left it here for me. I was worrying about your reaction to Billy seeming to be gay."

"It does help. I know that many of the stronger powers use sex as an energy source. I think a large part of the power might be tied to bi-sexuality.

"Cliff, I wouldn't care if he's gay. I've never been against what is basically a person's genetic inheritance. I would only worry about AIDS and such, though I think that a true power can guard against that kind of thing.

"I would prefer that he was straight, of course. It wouldn't overly concern me, if he's not.

"You do realize that Azterifat is here to protect me?"

"Both of us, I think." Gordy nodded.

They sailed into Kingston on a beautiful clear afternoon, to find Mama Bernadine waiting on the dock for them. Cliff was about to ask how she knew they were coming, when she said, "Gordon called me. I *do* sometimes use the telephone, mon! It ain't always the magic stuff."

They laughed, and headed for a little cantina downharbor in. Gordy asked her about Azterifat.

"How you know 'is name, mon?"

"He told me."

"Yah. He's got some powers I don't know. He weren't from me, you guessed, right, mon?"

"Tell us what you know about Billy," Gordy said.

"Billy who, mon?"

"Billy Hunter," Cliff said.

She grinned. "I don't know nothin' 'bout Billy Hunter. He done come here and tell me you is comin' and that I needs to give you Azterifat. He swore it were no contra. It were for you safety, mon. You and his father, he said."

"It has protected us," Gordy replied. "We think of it as a friend."

"Yah. Is."

"He didn't say anything about his mother?" Gordy asked. "She didn't have a message for him to give me?"

"Why she do that, mon? She give you message herself, in person." She pointed to a table to the side, where a woman was sitting.

"This was to get me to meet her and Billy?" Gordy asked, standing.

"No, mon. She do that later. After she no need power. She know bad omen with, you and she afraid. She love you, mon."

Gordy went to the table, and stood a second. The attractive woman slowly stood, and he was suddenly embracing her.

"Let's you and me go somewhere else so they don't have to, mon."

Mama Bernadine and Cliff went to another cantina, a short way away. She said she didn't have a glass to be empty, mon. Yet.

Cliff bought her a rum, and had one himself. This was as weird as anything he had even ever wondered about. He was in the middle of voodoo and witchcraft, and a lot of things he always thought were bullshit, until a very few days ago. He was even talking to a juju!

He thought about it. A very few days ago, he would have fought to the death to keep from being fucked by another man, now he had been. Willingly, apparently. He had, also apparently, found it pleasant! He had thought the jujus and spells were crap, all the way, now he knew for a fact that part of it was very real.

Didn't he? Could this all be trickery?

He didn't see how.

The boredom was gone. He had that. Real or imaginary, this had served a purpose for him.

Was he possessed by some kind of power Billy had planted in him? A power he didn't know was there, inside him?

"Mama, what happens now with Gordy and his love?"

"He still love her?"

"Oh, yeah!"

"She give up her power for him. She love him why she here."

"Why will she have to give up her power? I don't understand that."

"She have no power if she give it to him. He have no power to give to her. Billy, he have the power, strong. You know that. He fuck you, and you do what he say, and don't even know! Gordy, he fuck Maribel, and no have power to put. You see?"

"No way, but I'll take your word for it. Will she lose all her powers?"

"No, mon. She still be powerful, in some way. She talk with dead. That, maybe stay. She make medicine. That stay, 'cause ain't no power you need for it.

"Is something maybe she tell Gordy, mon. Is something maybe the dead tell her. He in great danger from something. It deadly danger an' evil if she give up power for him. She love him, mon.

"Mama Bernadine's glass done got empty."

They talked for more than an hour more, then Cliff went back to the boat, to find Billy on the deck. His hair was long and thick. No more Rasta braids. The children were in awe of him. He was talking with Azterifat, asking it about things only the children could know, then telling them.

"Welcome aboard!" Cliff greeted. "Your father and mother are discussing old times. I'd like to know a few things. Like what the hell is going on here!"

Billy laughed. "We're trying to save his soul and yours from hell, believe it or not."

"I don't believe in hell, so I suppose not."

"Hell isn't a place. It's a place."

Why did that make sense to him? "It's a place inside?"

"Yes and no. It's inside now, but it comes from outside."

"Where outside?"

"That's what we have to know. We weren't told. That means it's from a powerful place."

Cliff nodded. "Come on inside, and I'll fix something."

"Ah! Wanna fuck?"

"No, but it's not out of the question. Anymore."

Billy laughed. "I have to use it. I decided I might as well enjoy it. I really do, but I don't look for it. I don't want to get fucked, and I don't want to fuck you. That could change, so be careful! I get what I want!"

"I can't believe I'm joking about this. I can't believe a lot of things that are happening."

Cliff made a lobster chowder he particularly liked. They had a good meal, and talked for a long time, on the deck. They went to bed, about one in the morning, Billy in the second bunk. They talked a bit more there, then slept.

In the morning, just after sunrise, Gordy came aboard as Cliff and Billy were having coffee and an omelet.

"Ah, Gordy!" Cliff greeted. "I'd like for you to meet someone. Gordy, your son, Billy. Billy, your father, Gordon, called Gordy."

"I'll call him Dad," Billy answered. "I suppose he'll call me what Mother does. You Damned Little Snit!"

They laughed. "Your mother loves you more than life," Gordy replied. "I think I love her more than life, so it transfers to you.”

“Well, Maribel says we have to find someone, and that you probably have the power. You won’t be blocked like we are. Even Mama Bernadine doesn’t have the latent power.”

“I do?”

“Yes. It’s only seeking. I gave it to you because you won’t be blocked, like I am,” Billy replied.

“We have to know the source of the blocking, then we have to know if it was a borrowed source. If it was, it’s damned powerful, as those things go.”

“Borrowed?”

“The way I planted the power in you to involve Dad.”

Cliff didn’t begin to understand what they were saying, so didn’t pursue it. “Where do we go from here?” he asked.

“You tell us.”

“How? Just pick a place?”

“Ask Azterifat,” Gordy suggested. “As I understand it, Azterifat is a familiar to you.”

Cliff felt like a fool, but went on deck to ask Azterifat where they should go, now. Nothing. He went back inside, to find a navigation chart had fallen on the deck from the shelf. He picked it up, and looked at the chart.

"Santa Anita. I think Gordy and I should go. Not you or your mother."

"Why?" from Billy.

"I don't have a clue."

"Then it's best we don't go."

"I have one question about it," Cliff said. "Where the hell is Santa Anita? I never heard of it!"

Gordy got the big Atlas, and went through it, to discover there were dozens of Santa Anitas. Billy suggested it was on the water charts. Probably close.

"Santa Anita Island? Off the lower coast of Honduras, down near Nicaragua?" Gordy asked.

"Yes!" Cliff and Billy said, at once.

"Close enough to here. There are nothing but Mesquitu Indios in that area.

"Oh, shit!" Gordy exclaimed. "Maybe I know about where it's coming from! I worked with the Mesquitu for awhile!"

"You pissed off a voodoo priest there?" Cliff asked.

"No. I helped a voodoo priest there fight off a man from Louisiana – where Maribel and Billy are from!"

"Does the name Dihiti mean anything to you?" Billy asked.

"Yes. He was the priest. Why?"

"He's dead. He's the one who told Mom there was a deadly serious curse on you and on anyone who helped you."

"Simon D'Arginon!?" Gordy spat. "He's the one I helped Dihiti fight! He was supposedly lost at sea when he ran from Bahargui!"

"He, apparently, wasn't. You have the strength to fight him. He won't know who you are. Maybe Gordy shouldn't go with you."

The chart fell off the table. Cliff leaned over to see a fly light on a tiny island to the east of Santa Anita. Isla de las Piedras.

"Should we go there, or leave Gordy there?" Cliff asked.

The fly flew toward Santa Anita and returned to Isla de las Piedras.

"You leave Gordy there. Thank you Azterifat," Billy said. "I'll go to be with Mom. She's staying with Mama Bernadine. We can leave a lot of power with you."

"What? I've got to get fucked by a bunch of your friends?" Cliff asked.

Billy laughed. "Not this time. It's a different kind of transfer. If you want, I'll get a bunch of guys to fuck you. Me first!"

They joked a bit. Cliff felt good that these were people who could find humor in what was probably a deadly serious matter.

Billy soon left. Gordy and Cliff got the boat ready, and headed for the Honduran coast. Cliff gave the juju sugar, and talked to it. Gordy studied a lot of things on his computer.

It took two days and a night. They approached Isla de las Piedras just at the dawning. There was virtually nothing there, at all. It was, as the name suggested, a pile of rocks in the ocean. There were a few stunted trees, and some vines.

"I'll eat well! There have to be thousands of langosta around this place!" Gordy cried. "I have the radio, and I have the computer. I'll take the small gasolene generator and a few gallons of fuel. I have the bedroll, and a tent. I'll be fairly content, here, so long as you aren't gone more than two hours.

"Cliff, you're in the most serious danger you've ever faced in your life. You have a lot of power directed to your safety, but there's as much or more focused on the opposite. Take care!

"Billy, Mama Bernadine, and Maribel did something to Azterifat. I don't know what, but it may be that you can communicate with them through it, somehow.

"A lot of this is probably some kind of wild psy power. I don't know what to tell you about how to resist it. The way we got rid of

D'Arginon was to turn his power back on itself. Dihiti was able to do that. I can't help, this time. I don't know how. Dihiti was one who exhibited powers I couldn't explain."

Cliff nodded, and helped Gordy unload his things, including a rifle and a lot of smaller weapons. There was a little juju among them that Gordy didn't even know was there. It could have been put there by Maribel, or it could be from something else. He told Cliff to wait. He contacted Billy through the computer, and found that none of them knew anything about the juju.

"Put it close to Azterifat," Maribel ordered. "Put it close, and leave the boat for ten minutes."

Cliff didn't question that. He put the juju on the rail, just under Azterifat, and went onto the island to finish setting up Gordy's camp spot. When he went back aboard the boat, the juju was gone. He said, "Thanks. What did you do?"

He thought of a piece of plank, with the juju on it, going north on the tidal current.

"It was a locator? No more?"

There was the second slight movement that could have been a nod.

He moved off the island, and set sail to head for Santa Anita. It was about three hours away. Sailing was easy until very close, then there were flats and shallows. There didn't seem to be much on the island, except a few huts and a dock. He had to stand off the dock a ways, because it was too shallow. He used the dinghy to go to the dock. The old man sitting there said the sailboat could go to the dock on the far side of the island. The water was about four meters deep, there, at low tide.

The island was only about half a mile across by three quarters of a mile long, and had a hill, about fifteen meters high, in the center. It was ringed with coconut palms and sabals.

He went back to the boat and headed around the island. He saw the dock, and saw that there were several people waiting there. One was a gringo, by the looks of him.

Cliff tied the boat as four people came onto the long dock. They came close. One of them saw Azterifat and squealed. They all ran back off the dock.

What the hell was that about?

Cliff went aground, and walked along the path from the dock to where the group of people were waiting. The stranger explained that they were superstitious, saw the doll on his boat, and thought it was a vengeful devil, or something such. The man who had squealed and started the exodus said something about Dihiti. Cliff wouldn't let on that he had ever heard of any Dihiti.

"I am called Dr. Simon, here. It's a Phd, not medical. From the Louvre. I am studying the psychology of these people. They hear 'doctor' and assume it's medical, so I've learned a bit of first aid type of medicine.

"To what do we owe the honor of your presence, here?"

"I'm Cliff. No doctor or anything. I'm doing some research on Caribbean native medicines."

He decided to drop a bomb, and see how they reacted.

"Maybe you've heard of Dr. Hunter, from the states? I'm helping him with things like *Melia* and albaricoque. I imagine you've come across those in studying medicines."

He flinched ever so slightly, and nodded. "For parasites. Yes."

"Well, he told me to drop in on all the islands around here, because some local witch doctor had planted the *Melia* on some of them. It can become a problem, because it grows so fast, with no natural controls, and can take over an island."

"I take it there are no supply stores here?"

"No. Maybe someone comes once in two or three months."

"I don't think Utila is close?"

"Utila? No. Up closer to Rotan."

"Well, I'll stay here tonight, and clean up my notes, then head on up to the north. There doesn't seem to be anything here except rocks. Not very useful on a sailboat!"

"Yes. Well, we have little to offer guests. We do have some good coconut wine they make that is surprisingly quite tasty. Would you care for some before you return to your craft?"

He had been warned about that, and had a pill Gordy had given him to counteract on the hypnotic drug in it. He said that might well be a good idea. It was getting dark, and he didn't have much on the boat. He had hoped there would be a supply store on the island.

The wine was tasty. He drank enough that it should act in about twenty more minutes. He bid farewell, and went back aboard. He gave Azterifat the sugar, and went inside.

Half an hour later, he heard someone on the deck. He waited. D'Arginon stuck his head into the galley, and said, "Hello." Cliff returned a slurred hello. D'Arginon came inside.

"You will answer all questions rapidly and truthfully.

"Where is Dr. Hunter now?"

"Haiti. Or maybe Jamaica."

"What does he know of the people here?"

"I don't know. He said he was here."

"Did he mention anyone specific?"

"No. Maybe. A French name. I didn't pay attention."

"You will return to him soon?"

"In four or five months."

"Did he say anything about a son?"

"No. Not his son."

"He has a son, living in Louisiana. His name is William. Has he mentioned him? William? Bill?"

"No. He doesn't have any children."

"Did he ever mention Maribel?"

"I don't ... I'm not sure."

"Did he ever mention Dihiti?"

"I don't know where that is."

"It was a person we both knew."

Cliff didn't say anything.

"There is a powerful juju over the plank. Is it from Hunter?"

"The doll? It's from Mama Bernadine."

"It is to protect you from evil. It is powerful."

"It is a doll. I like it there. The children won't steal from the boat while it's there."

"Sleep!"

D'Arginon moved around the galley. He put something in the water jug, and went outside. A sudden lethargy came over Cliff. He couldn't move. There were terrible screams from the fore deck. D'Arginon came running into the galley, and a huge man came to grab him around the neck and throw him back onto the deck. There were more screams. There were noises, then there was silence.

Where had Cliff seen that huge man? He was very familiar. His face ... Azterifat?

Cliff went into a deep dark sleep. He woke up to discover the water jug had been smashed. He remembered something about it, but couldn't quite remember what it was.

He staggered to his feet, and went out onto the deck. There was blood everywhere.

Screams? He'd heard screams? Azterifat was

in the cabin?

He looked up at Azterifat. There was blood all over it.

"Azterifat! What happened?! Why ... Azterifat? Can you hear me?"

He had always felt that Azterifat could hear him, before. Now, it was like there was nothing there to hear. It was a doll.

He felt a great loss, and went dazedly onto the dock. There was blood in a trail that went to the far side. D'Arginon's body was there, impaled on a slender pole in the water.

The people at the end of the dock were edging slowly out toward him. He called that the danger was past. The evil demon-man was dead.

They came out, and stared at D'Arginon's body. The one who had squealed the night before went to the boat, and looked at Azterifat.

"He is not here, now. Dihiti, our mentor and friend, thank you, wherever you are."

He turned, and went down the dock, where he turned again to Cliff.

"Dihiti has removed the evil he brought you here to help him fight. You are a good man, and will always be a friend. It is better you go, now. Please do not ever tell anyone about this, unless you say it was somewhere else, and with other people. It is evil, and it is gone."

"You have Dr. Hunter and his son and Mama Bernadine to thank for bringing Dihiti here," Cliff said. "Only they will hear anything about this."

"Yes. Dihiti showed that he had warned the mother of Gordon's good son that he was in great danger."

"He communicated with you?"

"With Mama Dona. She speaks sometimes with the dead."

Cliff nodded. He didn't want to know more. He washed the blood from the deck of his boat, then set sail to pick up Gordy. They then went back to Jamaica, to Maribel, Billy, and Mama Bernadine. Maribel was a striking, dark woman.

They sat around the sala to discuss what had happened. Cliff wanted desperately to separate fact from fancy. He didn't want to believe much of this wild adventure.

"It started when I was channeling with Ninoeth Mantingo, a black African priest who died in seven hundred twenty nine," Maribel said.

"Mom!" Billy warned. They all laughed.

"I sometimes have some kind of communication with people who died with a heavy burden on their souls. There has to be another connection with me, of course. Gordon was and is that connection, reinforced by Billy.

"Dihiti was a strong psychic, with some power to move things. He has imparted some of that to Billy. He died with a belief that D'Arginon had tricked them. He sought and found him, and found he was insane in seeking revenge against Gordon for thwarting his attempt to control the people of the Mesquitu. He had returned there after Dihiti's death, and was terrorizing the people. He was plotting to find and destroy Gordon.

"D'Arginon found about Billy and me through another writer of psychic things. Liam revealed about us, in innocence. He knew, from not long after Billy was born. He helped us, for a time. He agreed that he would not let Gordon know of Billy.

"D'Arginon uses hypnotic drugs in his studies. Quite by accident, he used them on Liam, and as accidentally asked the question that would make him reveal about us.

"D'Arginon had powers. He blocked Billy and myself. Liam had spoken of Bernadine, and he blocked her, because of what she might be able to relate.

"Bernadine has a strong natural power that isn't educated, so the blockage was only a partial one. Dihiti found it, and traced, then communicated with the psychic part of her mind. He had her make a juju that would be given to a friend of Gordon.

"Dihiti put himself into that juju. It was he who took his revenge against D'Arginon. It was he who made Cliff sleep through the many horrors he visited on D'Arginon.

"It was on his instructions that Billy came here and to Haiti to help prepare and strengthen Cliff. Had Cliff failed in helping Dihiti, Gordon would necessarily be called. Dihiti had the good spirits to help. I thank them that they were able to keep Gordon away from the horror.

"There is a balance. It is restored. We may now pass forward. I will spend the rest of my life with the one person I have loved totally these twenty years."

"You will lose your power, but that is perhaps to the good," Mama Bernadine decided.

"I have passed my powers to my son. There is balance."

"Do you have anymore questions, Cliff?" Gordy asked.

"Thousands, but I can live with the ones I have. It's become one hell of a way to fight boredom. I think I want to know if that idea was from outside."

"Yes. You were bored, but not to the extent you believed," Maribel answered. "Dihiti needed a friend of Gordon who was strong and intelligent. He couldn't find one, so settled for you."

They laughed. "I have to admit I learned a lot about myself. I'm not at all what I thought I was. I think I like me better the way I am than the way I was."

"We has to shed all that shit about what we's *supposed* to think," Mama Bernadine said. "We's *supposed* to think different from what is nature. When we thinks like is real nature we can be happy. Can't never happen if we's all phony-face.

"Gordy, what you gonna do with that lady in you house?"

"Well, she has to help Maribel with the housework, if she stays! That's only right!

"Seriously, we're comfortable. We aren't in love, or any of that. We never planned for it to last forever. I think she wants a younger man to sleep with. Maybe Billy."

"Nah-ah!" Billy cried. "Then I'd have to sneak around on Cliff!"

There are times for good friends to relax and be silly. This was one of them.

C. D. Moulton's works are available on most major outlets as printed or e-books. CD writes the CD Grimes, PI mysteries, the Det. Lt. Nick Storie mysteries, the Clint Faraday mysteries, the Flight of the Maita science fiction series, books on orchid culture and many others of many types. Mystery, adventure, intrigue, science fiction, fantasy, paranormal, mild erotica, and factual.

www.ingramcontent.com/pod-product-compliance
Lightning Source LLC
Chambersburg PA
CBHW052229150726
48002CB00003B/1345